Tom Goes to Kindergarten

Margaret Wild

David Legge

Albert Whitman & Company
Morton Grove, Illinois

For Teresa and Zoran.
— M.W.

For Callum.
— D.L.

Library of Congress Cataloging-in-Publication Data

Wild, Margaret, 1948 —
   Tom goes to kindergarten / by Margaret Wild;
illustrated by David Legge
   p. cm.
Summary: When Tom, a young panda, goes to his very
first day of kindergarten, his whole family stays and
plays and wishes they could be in kindergarten too.
   ISBN 0-8075-8012-0
[1. Pandas — Fiction. 2. Kindergarten — Fiction. 3.
First day of school — Fiction. 4. Schools — Fiction.]
I. Legge, David, 1963 — ill. II. Title.
   PZ7.W64574 Tr 2000
   [E] — dc21   99-050420

First published in Australia in 1999 by ABC Books.

Text copyright © 1999 by Margaret Wild.
Illustrations copyright © 1999 by David Legge.
Published in 2000 by Albert Whitman & Company,
6340 Oakton Street, Morton Grove, Illinois
60053-2723.
Published simultaneously in Canada by General
Publishing, Limited, Toronto.
Printed in Hong Kong.
10 9 8 7 6 5 4 3 2

The illustrations are rendered in watercolor.
The typeface is 23/35 Bembo.
Designed and typeset by Monkeyfish.

Every day, Tom and his mother and Baby went past
kindergarten on their morning walk.

"That'll be *you* soon, Tom,"
his mother said.

Tom thought, "Yes! That's me building
a spaceship! That's me being a king!
That's me making a monster!"

When they got home, Tom wanted his mother to be an astronaut or a princess or a googly monster. But first she had laundry to hang up, plants to water, and dishes to wash.

So Tom was the googly monster, and he dressed Baby up as a princess.

When his father came home from work, Tom jumped on him and said, "Let's play spaceships!"

But his father said, "In a while," because first he had to take out the recycling bin, cook dinner, and iron some shirts.

So Tom was an astronaut, and Baby was a creature from outer space.

One morning — at long last — it was time for Tom to start kindergarten.

"Yes!"

said Tom.

The whole family went with him
to kindergarten. Tom pushed
open the gate, leaped up the steps, and
there, waiting for him, was Mrs. Polar Bear.

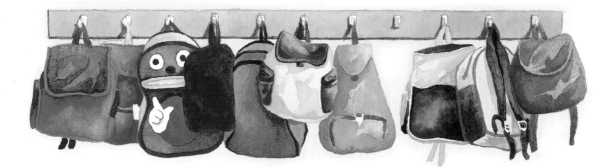

Mrs. Polar Bear showed Tom
where to put his backpack, and she
found him two new friends.

Tom hugged his father, kissed his
mother three times, then hugged
his father again.

"Have a good time, Tom,"
said his father.

"I'll come get you later this
afternoon," said his mother.

Suddenly, Tom didn't want them to
leave. He grabbed his father's left
leg and his mother's right leg,
and wouldn't let go.

Mrs. Polar Bear said,
"If you like, Mr. and Mrs. Panda,
you can stay for today."

"Er, well, um ..."
said Tom's mother.

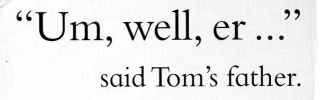

"Um, well, er ..."
said Tom's father.

"Yes!" said Tom.

"Please?"

So his father and mother and Baby stayed for the day.

They played in the sandbox,

and in the
dress-up corner.

They painted a picture,

listened to a story,

and sang, "I'm a little teapot, short and stout."

In the afternoon, they raced home to put their paintings on the fridge. And when dinner was over, they turned the dining room table into a castle.

"Do you like kindergarten, Tom?" asked his mother.

"I LOVE kindergarten!" said Tom.

"Me too," said his father.

"And me, too," said his mother, but she spoke so softly, only Baby heard.

The next day at kindergarten, Tom hugged his
father, kissed his mother three times,
and then hugged his father again.

"Goodbye, Daddy and Mommy
and Baby," said Tom.

But they didn't
want to go.

"Don't you want to grab my left leg?" asked Tom's father.

"Don't you want to grab my right leg?" asked Tom's mother.

"No," said Tom.

And he skipped away to see what Mrs. Polar Bear was doing.

Tom's father and mother and Baby

skipped after him.

"We're going to make sailor hats today,"
said Mrs. Polar Bear. "Won't that be fun?"

"Yes!"

said Tom.

"Yes!"

said his father.

"Yes!"

said his mother.

And they all hurried over to the dress-up corner
to find some baggy pants and some sailor scarves.

"Don't you have to go to work?" asked Mrs. Polar Bear.

"Er, well, um ..."
said Tom's mother.

"Um, well, er ..."
said Tom's father.

And they took off their baggy
trousers, and they took off
their sailor scarves.

"Goodbye, Daddy and
Mommy and Baby," said Tom,
feeling sorry for them.

Tom's mother went home
and paid the bills and
washed the windows
and weeded the garden.

Tom's father went to the office
and signed a lot of papers
and made a lot of phone calls.

Then ... Tom's mother and Baby made a ship!

Baby was an excellent pirate.

And ... Tom's father closed the office door, made himself a sailor hat, sang a sailor song and —

hurried home to find out what Tom
had done at kindergarten that day.